NAUGHTY CATCOON
The Rascal Raccoon

written by Janice L. Dodson

illustrated by Trisha St.Clair

For information contact Picture Bright Books at picturebrightbooks@gmail.com
Library of Congress Cataloging-in-Publication Data
Dodson, Janice,   Naughty Catcoon.
Summary: Under the light of the moon, a rascal raccoon ransacks and romps in a child's backyard, wakes the child, and makes a mess before he scampers away.
[1.Raccoons-Fiction. 2. Animals-Fiction. 3. Nocturnal animals-Fiction.
4. Backyard play-Fiction. 5. Moonlit night-Fiction. 6. Stories in rhyme.]
Library of Congress Catalog Card Number 2018945810
ISBN 978-1-945526-42-8

J.L.D. For Grace who named our invading rascal raccoon "Catcoon" and her backyard playmates: her sister Charlotte and little cousins Colby, Oscar, Ivy, Catlyn, Mila and Lucas.

T.S.C. For Waterstreet, Brownfield, and McElroy - art instructors extraordinaire. And for my family and friends who encourage my artistic endeavors.

In the middle of the night,
a very starry night,
lit by the light of the moon,

and saw a dancing Catcoon.

I turned on the light
that was very bright
to make him run away.

But all that Catcoon did
was stop and stare
then continued to play.

He ate from the cat's dish

and tried to catch goldfish
from our backyard lagoon.
What a naughty Catcoon!

I pounded on the pane
and yelled, "Get out of here!"

He did not run away.
He did not disappear.

Then I could see him
as he climbed onto
the trampoline,

wobbled and bobbled
bouncing away.
What a silly scene.

He scampered towards the pool

and knocked over a stool

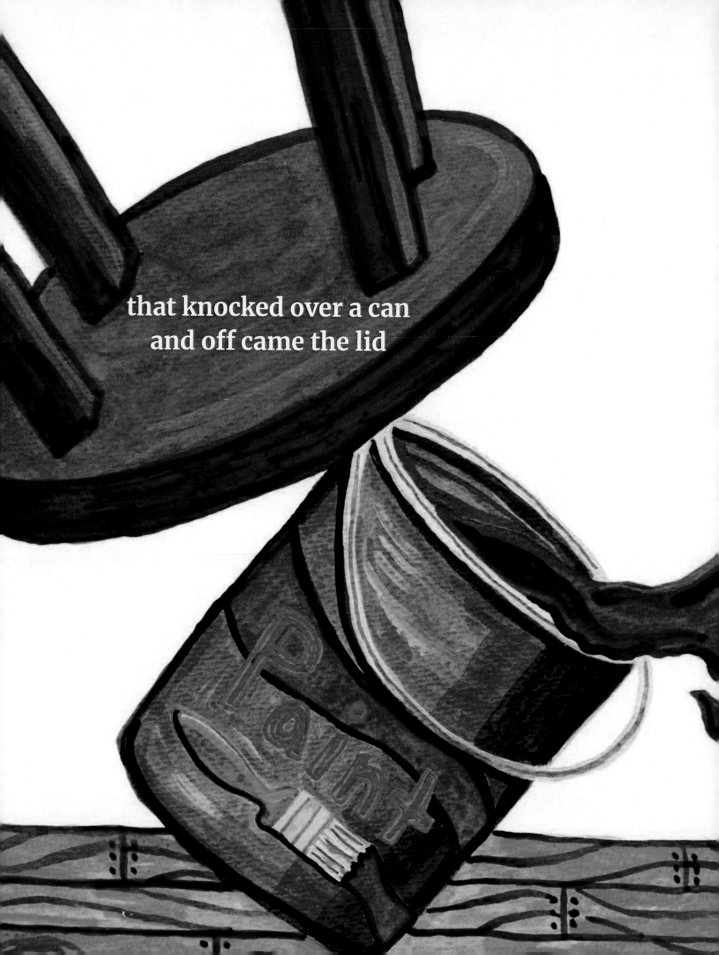

that knocked over a can
and off came the lid

then out poured purple paint
through which Catcoon slid.

What a naughty Catcoon!

What a mess that sassy
Catcoon made. What a fool!

Then he waddled on the
edge of the wading pool.

He took a long cool drink.

He pulled out our big pink
ball floating in the pool.

He pushed it and hit it.

He scratched it
and bit it.

He popped our ball.
Not cool!

What a naughty Catcoon!

Then after all that from our naughty brat
he scampered away out of my sight
into the shrubs and darkness of night.

I was glad he went. It was not too soon
to say goodbye to that naughty Catcoon!

For our naughty Catcoon
was a rascal raccoon,

and they ransack and romp
by the light of the moon.

Goodnight you naughty Catcoon!